An ANGEL Without WINGS

Written by Stacey J.S. Haggerty

~⅋

Illustrated by Manuela Pentangelo

Publishers Cataloging-in-Publication Data

Haggerty, Stacey J.S.
   An angel without wings / written by Stacey J.S. Haggerty ; illustrated
by Manuela Pentangelo.
   p. cm.
   Summary: Through verse and illustration, describes the love a mother
and father have for their new baby and their joy as they watch him grow.
   ISBN-13: 978-1-60131-055-2
   [1. Parent and child—Poetry. 2. Parent and child—Juvenile poetry.
3. Families—Poetry. 4. Families—Juvenile poetry. 5. Babies—Poetry.
6. Infants—Juvenile poetry.] I. Pentangelo, Manuela, ill. II. Title.
                                 2009934702

115 Bluebill Drive
Savannah, GA 31419
United States
(888) 300-1961

To order additional copies please go to **www.bigtentbooks.com**

This book was published with the assistance of the helpful folks at DragonPencil.com

To my greatest accomplishment, my son Joseph Anthony II;
and to every child blessed with the knowledge that he or she is
an angel without wings.

A beautiful sight on a warm summer's night

A beautiful sunshine when the skies are gray

A rainbow of colors to brighten up the day

A gift from Heaven, that's what you are

A love I thought I would never know

A beautiful face that I behold

In my heart is where you'll always be

A gift from Heaven, that's what you are

An angel without wings, placed in my care

My heart yearned to see your face

My arms longed for the warmth of your embrace

A gift from Heaven, that's what you are

An angel without wings, placed in my care

Someone to love, someone to hold and never let go
Someone to guide, someone to kiss
Someone to hug, someone to miss
A gift from Heaven, that's what you are
An angel without wings, placed in my care

When I heard your first cry
My heart gasped with delight
A gift from Heaven, that's what you are
An angel without wings, placed in our care

When I saw your face for the first time

It was the beginning of unspeakable joy

A gift from Heaven, that's what you are

An angel without wings, placed in our care

The first time I held you in my arms

Tears fell from my eyes

Tears of joy, tears of wonder, tears of delight

A gift from Heaven, that's what you are

An angel without wings, placed in my care

Our first kiss was magical

Time stood still, if only for a moment

A gift from Heaven, that's what you are

An angel without wings, placed in our care

You are my heart

You are my joy

A gift from Heaven, that's what you are

An angel without wings, placed in our care

When I look into your eyes

I see a pure and perfect world

A face full of delight, a heart filled with love

A gift from Heaven, that's what you are

An angel without wings, placed in our care

You are me and I am you

You are we and we are you

A gift from Heaven, that's what you are

An angel without wings, placed in my care

We are your safe haven, we are your truth
Our love created you
Our love will forever be with you
A gift from Heaven, that's what you are
An angel without wings, placed in our care

You are beautiful and special in every way
You have blessed us more than words can say
A gift from Heaven, that's what you are
An angel without wings, placed in our care

I loved you yesterday, before you came to be

I love you today, because of who you are

I will love you tomorrow, for all you mean to me

A gift from Heaven, that's what you are

An angel without wings, placed in my care

We are different but still the same

We are Mommy and Daddy

That will never change

A gift from Heaven, that's what you are

An angel without wings, placed in our care

Someday we will have to go

But know that you will never be alone

Look inside yourself and you will see

That we are you and you are we

A gift from Heaven, that's what you are

An angel without wings, placed in our care